D0543276

This Little Tiger book

belongs to:

_____

_____

_____

To Millie Grace and Darcy Mae Rogers

LITTLE TIGER PRESS LTD,
an imprint of the Little Tiger Group
1 Coda Studios, 189 Munster Road, London SW6 6AW
www.littletiger.co.uk

First published in Great Britain 2014
This edition published 2018
Text and illustrations copyright © Tim Warnes 2014
Visit Tim Warnes at www.ChapmanandWarnes.com
Tim Warnes has asserted his right to be identified as the author and
illustrator of this work under the Copyright, Designs and Patents Act, 1988
A CIP catalogue record for this book is available from the British Library
All rights reserved

CD contains:
1 - complete story with original music and sound effects
2 - story with page turn pings to encourage learner readers to join in

Running time over 15 mins
Music composed by Christopher Sarantis
Story read by Anna Crace
This recording copyright © Little Tiger Press 2018
℗ Christopher Sarantis

All rights of the producer and owner of the recorded work reserved.
Unauthorised public performance, broadcasting, copying and
hiring of this recording prohibited.

ISBN 978-1-78881-027-2
LTP/1900/2310/0418
Printed in China
2 4 6 8 10 9 7 5 3

Mole loved labelling things.
All sorts of things.
Anything really.
   Naming things was
what Mole liked best.

One day, Mole found something unusual on the path.

"What is THIS strange thing?" he wondered.

He poked it gently.
Then he stuck a
label on it: lumpy.

And another: bumpy . . .

. . . and then a few more.
But he still didn't know
what it was.

SUDDENLY...

...the **enormous** **Lumpy-Bumpy Thing** gave a **big** stretch and yawned **a terrifying**

But the **Lumpy-Bumpy Thing**
just rolled over and went back
to sleep.

Mole peered out from the bushes.

"That thing looks dangerous!" he whispered. "Somebody might get hurt." He scribbled out another label. Then he crept, oh-so-carefully, over to the sleeping beast.

The **LUMPY-BUMPY Thing** licked its long, scaly lips, flashed its snippy-snappy teeth and . . .

...gobbled up all the labels!

Yum! Yum! Yum!

"Stop that!" cried Mole.
"You can't eat them!"

And he stomped off

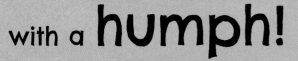

with a **humph!**

But wherever Mole went, the
Lumpy-Bumpy Thing went too.

It wanted to play...

No, thank you!

Boo!

It thought Mole was
wonderful!

Go AWAY!

Mole did not feel the same way at all. And the **Lumpy-Bumpy Thing** was **still** gobbling labels!

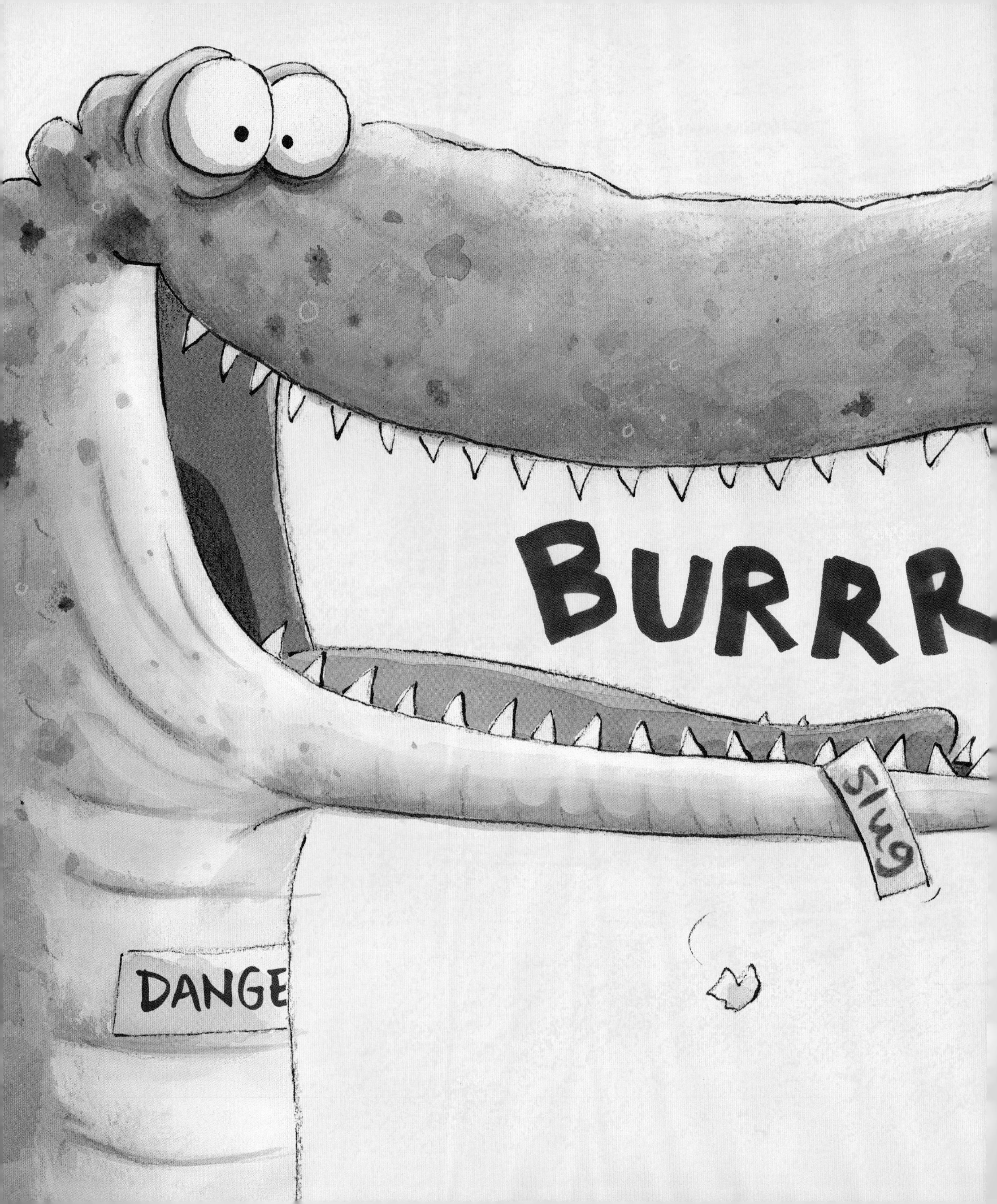
BURRR
slug
DANGE

"That does it!" yelled Mole.
"You're a slurpy,

burpy,

lumpy,

bumpy,

greedy,

naughty...

THING!"

RRP!!!

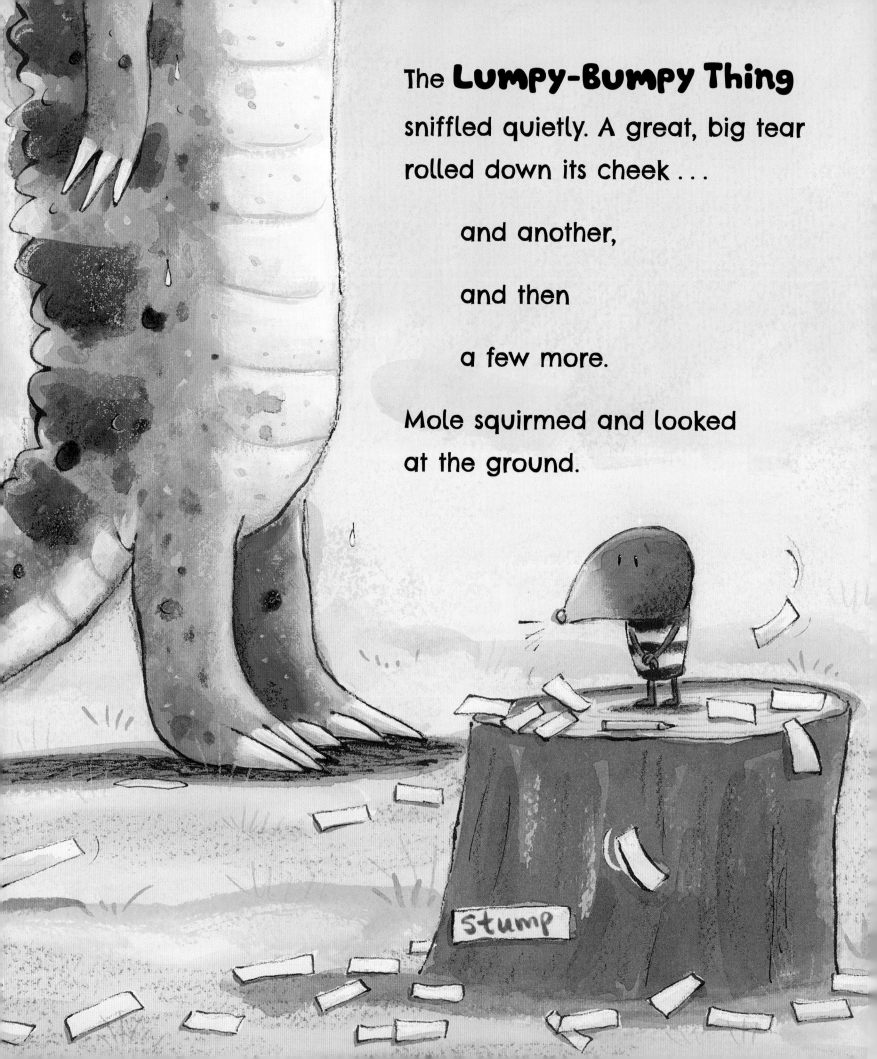

The **Lumpy-Bumpy Thing** sniffled quietly. A great, big tear rolled down its cheek . . .

and another,

and then

a few more.

Mole squirmed and looked at the ground.

stump

The **Lumpy-Bumpy Thing**
stuck
a label
to its
tummy: sorry.

"I'm sorry too," said Mole.
There was a bit of an
awkward silence.
Then he scribbled down
a brand new word . . .

FRIEND!

More fabulous books from Little Tiger Press!

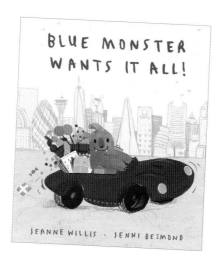

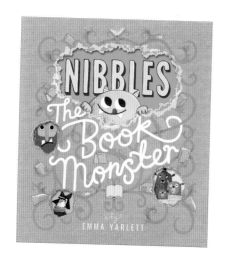

For information regarding any of the above books or for our catalogue, please contact us:
Little Tiger Press, 1 Coda Studios, 189 Munster Road, London SW6 6AW
Tel: 020 7385 6333 • E-mail: contact@littletiger.co.uk • www.littletiger.co.uk

Image taken from *Big, Bad Owl* copyright © Richard Watson 2014